THE SHIPWRECKED SAILOR

TAMARA BOWER
THE SHIPWRECKED SAILOR
AN EGYPTIAN TALE WITH HIEROGLYPHS

ATHENEUM BOOKS FOR YOUNG READERS

New York London Toronto Sydney Singapore

Special thanks to Melinda Hartwig for translating the hieroglyphs for this book.
She is a graduate of the Institute of Fine Arts, New York University, in Near Eastern Art
and Archaeology, with an emphasis in Egyptian Art.

I would like to thank my editor, Marcia Marshall, my art director, Ann Bobco,
and the following people: Diane Bergman, Brenda Bowen, Devin Bower, William Bower,
Angela Carlino, Mary Flower, Laura Godwin, Mary Gow, Steve Harvey, Deb Kayman,
Sam Kayman, Sidney Levit, Kevin Lewis, Ann Martin, Faith Morgan, Jim Romano,
Richard Rosenblum, Catherine Siracusa, Donald Spanel, and Caitlin Van Dusen.

Atheneum Books for Young Readers
An imprint of Simon & Schuster Children's Publishing Division
1230 Avenue of the Americas
New York, New York 10020
Copyright © 2000 by Tamara Bower
Book design by Angela Carlino
The text of this book is set in Cantoria.
Printed in Hong Kong
2 4 6 8 10 9 7 5 3 1
Library of Congress Cataloging-in-Publication Data
Bower, Tamara.
The shipwrecked sailor: an Egyptian tale with hieroglyphs / retold and illustrated by Tamara Bower. — 1st ed.
p. cm.
Summary: A tale, based on a story found in ancient papyrus scrolls, about a shipwrecked sailor who finds fortune
when he is befriended by a serpent that is the Prince of the magical island of Punt.
ISBN 0-689-83046-7
[1. Folklore—Egypt.] I. Title.
PZ8.1.B667Sh   2000   398.2'0932'02—dc21   99-24821

FIRST
EDITION

For my brother, Devin:

This island will always be with you,

for it lives in your heart.

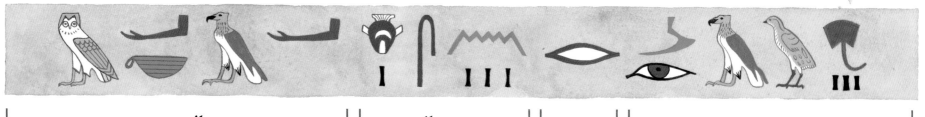

ma'ka		ib-sen	er	maw
fiercer		their hearts	than	lions

A ship is returning to Egypt after a long journey to Nubia. As the shoreline comes into view, the lieutenant turns to his commander and tells the tale of another voyage.

I was sailing the Red Sea on a great ship, 120 cubits long and 40 cubits wide, bound for the gold mines of Nubia. There were 120 of the best and bravest sailors of Egypt. There wasn't a fool among them. Their hearts were fiercer than lions. The arm of each one was stronger than the next, and the heart of each one was braver. They laughed at the thought of a storm!

But suddenly, a great wind arose, and a mighty wave dashed against our ship, breaking the mast. I grabbed hold of a piece of wood, and none too soon! The ship sank, and of those in it, I was the only one to survive.

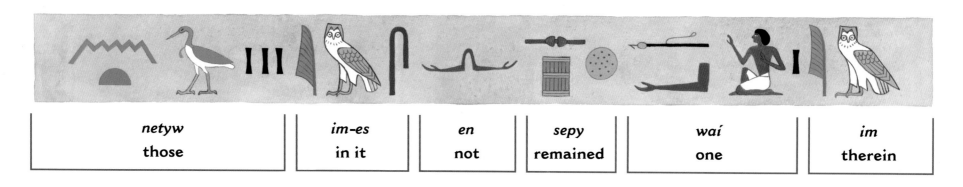

netyw	*im-es*	*en*	*sepy*	*waí*	*im*
those	in it	not	remained	one	therein

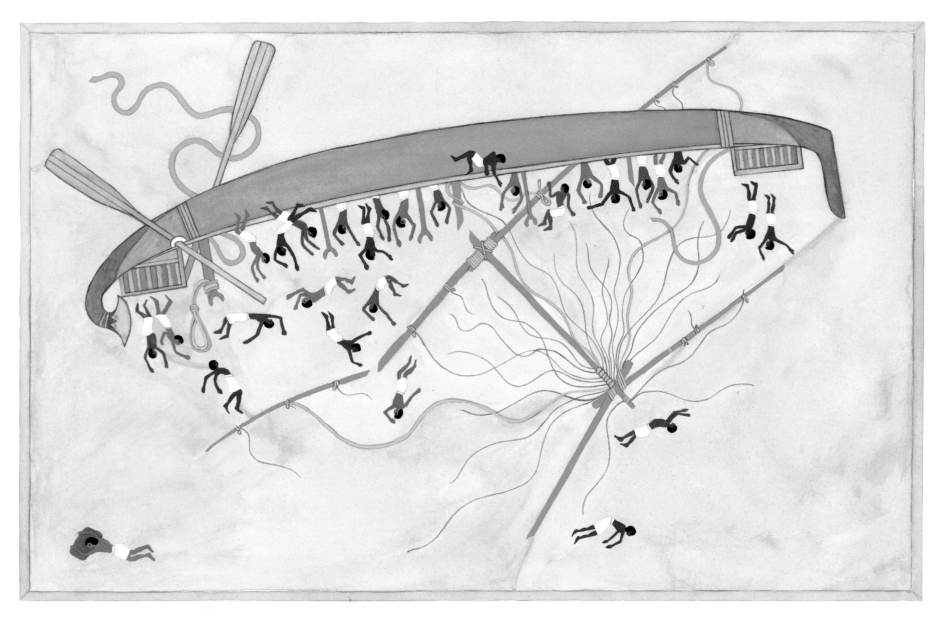

I floated until the surf cast me on an island shore. I crawled beneath some trees and fell asleep.

When I awoke, I found myself in a paradise. All around me were good things to eat: ripe figs, grapes, vegetables, grain, and an abundance of fish and wildfowl. I ate until I was full. Then I built a fire and made an offering to the gods, thanking them for my safety.

xewt	her gemgem	ta	her menmen
trees	splintered	ground	trembled

Then suddenly trees splintered and the ground trembled. I thought it was another storm, but I looked up and saw a gigantic Serpent, thirty cubits long, with a royal beard and scales of gold and lapis lazuli. The Serpent spoke, asking me, "Where are you from and how did you get here? Speak quickly, for if you do not answer me, I will spit fire and burn you to ashes!" I was so terrified I became speechless.

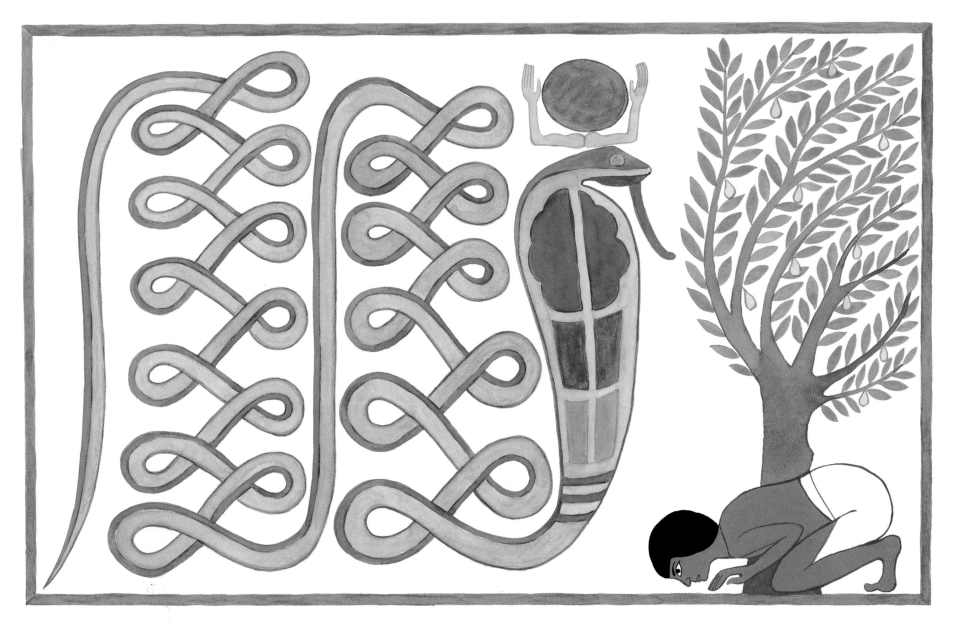

kem-en-en	nefaw	75 (not vocalized)
we amounted to	serpents	75

The Great Serpent picked me up in his mouth, carried me back to where he lived, and put me down again, unhurt. He said, "Fear not, I will not harm you. How have you come to this island?"

I told him I was on my way to Nubia when a storm destroyed our ship and all my companions were drowned.

"I know what it is like to lose companions," answered the Serpent. "I lived here with my sisters and brothers and all our children. We were seventy-five serpents living together in harmony and plenty, when one day a star fell from the sky and killed everyone except myself. So you and I are both survivors. How I miss my family!"

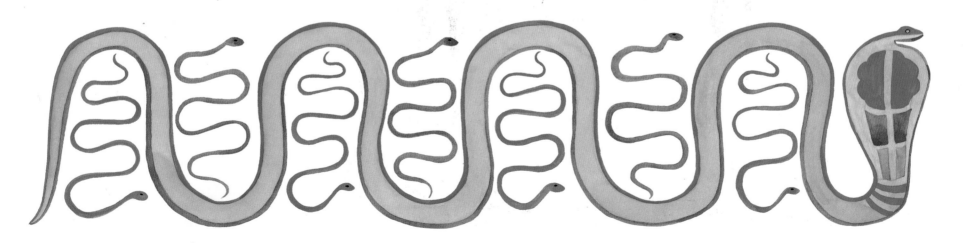

When he mentioned his family, I thought of my own wife and children and I wept.

"Grieve not," said the Serpent, "for good will come of your misfortune. You are safe here. You will stay here for four months, and then a ship will come filled with your countrymen who will return you to Egypt, and you will be reunited with your family."

How happy I was to hear this! "O Good Serpent, when I return to Egypt, I will tell Pharaoh of your kindness, wisdom, and hospitality, and we will send you gifts of gold, fragrant oil, and myrrh."

At this the Serpent laughed. "Little One, I have all the riches I need and more, for I am the Prince of Punt. Surely God brought you here to this Island of the Soul. When you leave, this island will disappear forever under the waves, but it will always be with you, for it lives in your heart. Whenever you face danger, take courage, and know that this island lives within you."

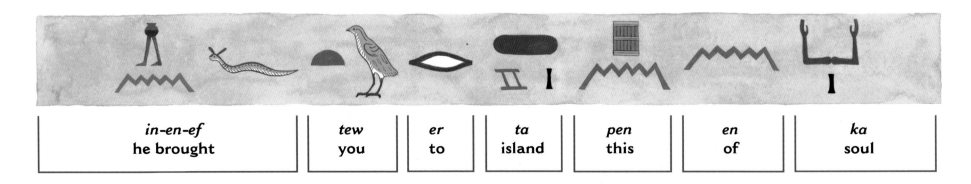

in-en-ef	tew	er	ta	pen	en	ka
he brought	you	to	island	this	of	soul

And so I lived with the Serpent, and we became good friends. In four months' time, a ship appeared. I climbed a tree to hail it and recognized Egyptians aboard.

When I went to tell the Serpent that the ship had arrived, he already knew. He said, "Farewell, Little One! You will reach your home in two months and embrace your wife and children. Speak well of me in your town and establish my good name. This is all I ask of you."

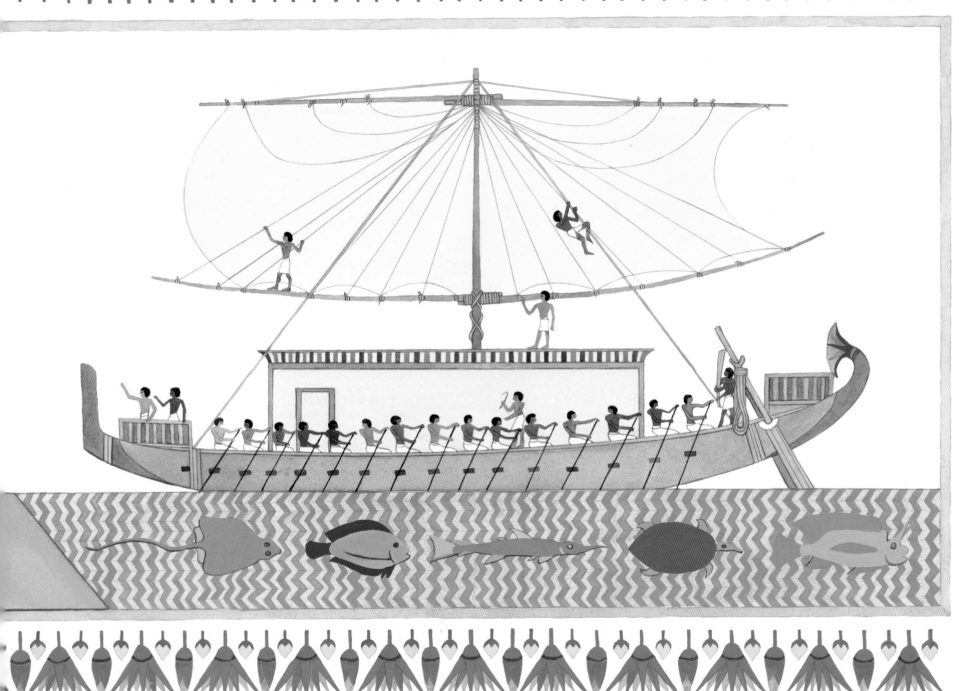

19

tjesemew greyhounds	gefew long-tailed monkeys	keyew baboons	shepsesew precious things	neb all	nefer good

The Good Serpent gave me many gifts, and we filled the ship with greyhounds, long-tailed monkeys, baboons, and all kinds of precious things.

I brought these gifts to Pharaoh, who rewarded me with a fine house, and appointed me lieutenant.

Then, as the Serpent predicted, I returned to my family. What a joy it was for us to be reunited!

| *keny-ek* you shall fill your embrace | *em* with | *kherdew-ek* your children | *sen-ek* you shall kiss | *hemet-ek* your wife | *ma-ek* you shall see | *per-ek* your home |

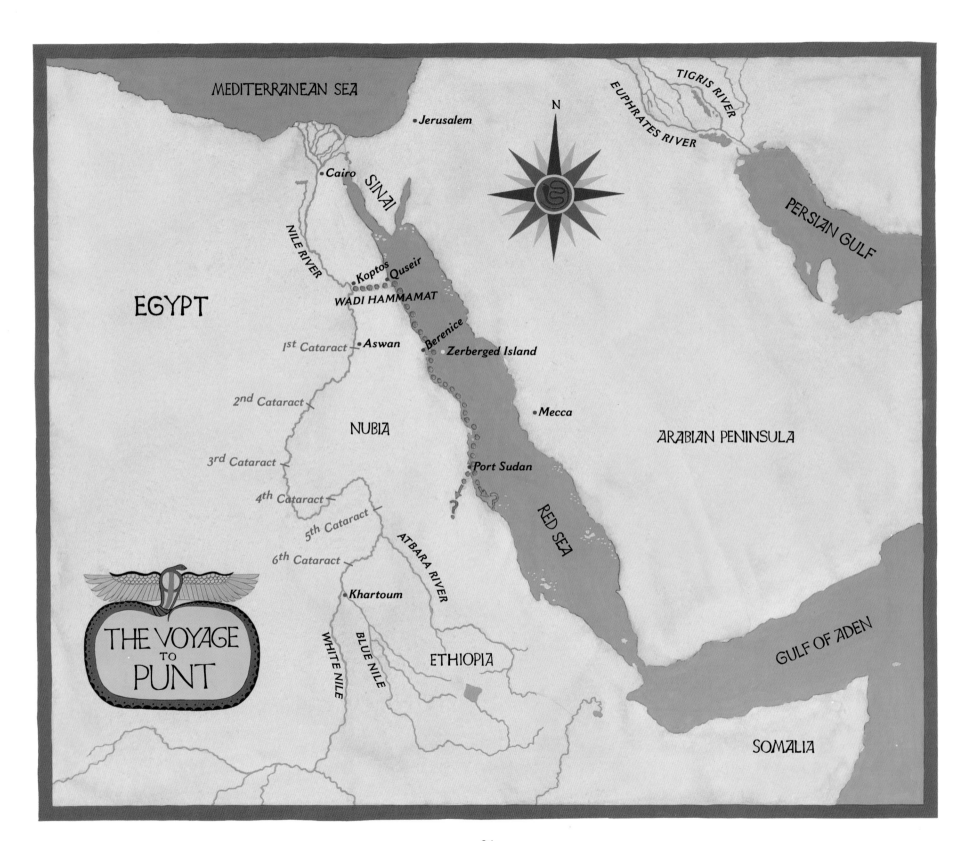

MEDITERRANEAN SEA

TIGRIS RIVER

EUPHRATES RIVER

Jerusalem

N

PERSIAN GULF

Cairo

SINAI

NILE RIVER

Koptos *Quseir*

WADI HAMMAMAT

EGYPT

1st Cataract *Aswan*

Berenice

Zerberged Island

2nd Cataract

NUBIA

Mecca

ARABIAN PENINSULA

3rd Cataract

Port Sudan

4th Cataract

5th Cataract

RED SEA

ATBARA RIVER

6th Cataract

THE VOYAGE TO PUNT

Khartoum

WHITE NILE

BLUE NILE

ETHIOPIA

GULF OF ADEN

SOMALIA

A NOTE ABOUT THIS STORY

This story is found in an ancient papyrus scroll in the Hermitage Museum in Moscow. It probably dates to the nineteenth century B.C., during the Middle Kingdom, the classical period of Egyptian literature.

It was during the Middle Kingdom that the Pharaohs Senwosret I, and later his grandson, Senwosret III, conducted military campaigns into Nubia (modern Sudan). They expanded Egyptian power and influence there and extended Egyptian control over Nubia's gold mines. The pharaohs also sent royal agents to explore new and profitable trade routes. We don't know exactly where the sailor in our story was going but most likely he was headed for Nubia or Punt.

South of Egypt, the Nile becomes difficult to sail because of dangerous stretches of rapids known as cataracts. There were six cataracts between Aswān in Egypt and Khartoum in Nubia. An alternate route to Nubia on the Red Sea would have avoided the cataracts.

Punt was a country south of Nubia from which Egypt obtained incense and other goods from central Africa. The Serpent calls himself the "Prince of Punt." Today we are not sure where Punt was. It may have been southern Nubia, Ethiopia, or Somalia.

Many scholars believe that this story is a fantasy or an allegory. However, the scholar Gerald A. Wainwright suggests that the Island of the Soul actually exists; that today it is called Zerberged and is off the coast near the town of Berenice, on the Red Sea. There are indeed legends from other ancient sources that tell of this island being inhabited by serpents, all of whom were destroyed by a catastrophe; and of the island being shrouded in mists and hard to find. There are often storms in this area.

The journey to Nubia and Punt was difficult and dangerous. From the town of Koptos on the Nile, the sailors marched over land for eight days through the Wadi Hammamat, a dry riverbed that runs across the desert to the Red Sea. The sailors had to carry the ship with them, and all the food

and supplies they would need for the long journey, plus goods for trade, such as honey, oil, and fine linen cloth. One inscription tells us that there were donkeys loaded just with extra sandals. The desert was very hot and dry, the men could not carry all the water they needed, so wells had been dug along the way. If the wells were dry, the men could die of thirst. There was also danger of attack by hostile nomadic tribes or bands of thieves.

The ship would have been built in the Nile Valley, and it was probably taken apart at Koptos so that it could be carried in pieces across the desert. Each part of the ship was marked with carpenters' symbols so they would know how the parts fit together. When the sailors reached the coast of the Red Sea, they put the ship back together. Egyptian sailors did not use nails, but held the planks together with wooden pegs and skillfully stitched ropes.

A cubit is an ancient measurement, the length of one arm from the elbow to the fingers. The ship in the story would have been about 200 feet long by 60 feet wide. The wave that destroyed it would have been about 13.5 feet high. It would have towered over a boat that lay low in the water and would have been a terrifying sight.

The crew set sail in summer when the winds and currents took them southward. It would take them about a month to reach Punt. They probably landed at what today is known as Port Sudan.

Once landed, the Egyptians probably marched across the sandy coastal plain to the foothills of the Red Sea Mountains and into Punt, about 250 miles inland. They would have had two or three months to gather the luxury goods they came for: incense trees, ebony, gold, and exotic animals.

In November or December, they again set sail as the currents changed direction to carry them north. The wind would blow north for only part of the way, but later on the sailors would have had to row with the current and against the wind. The return home took up to two months. Then they had to cross the harsh, dry desert again to reach the Nile Valley, protecting their precious cargo from bandits.

It was a brave sailor who made this journey.

EXPLANATION OF SYMBOLS

The paintings in this book are based on ancient Egyptian art, mostly on New Kingdom temple and tomb decorations.

There was a direct relationship between hieroglyphs and Egyptian art. Often figures and objects in a painted scene are represented in the same way as the hieroglyphs. Many works of art were meant to be "read" symbolically. The following list is a guide to some of the symbols and meanings contained in some of the paintings.

PAGE 7: The paintings of ships in this book are modeled after the ships in Queen Hatshepsut's temple at Deir el Bahri. This powerful ruler had sent an expedition to Punt.

PAGE 8: The symbol at the top of this page is the hieroglyph for the sky, covered with stars. The lines descending from the sky represent rain. As it rarely rains in Egypt, this hieroglyph was seldom used. The jagged yellow line, which resembles lightning, means darkness.

PAGE 12: The hieroglyph for life is given two human arms, which hold the symbols for dominion, the King's power to rule. They rest on alabaster bowls, which in this context mean "all," so that this common border design says "all life and dominion."

PAGE 13: On top of the Serpent's head are two human arms, which are the symbol for the soul. The Serpent lives on the Island of the Soul. In between the arms is a red disk representing the sun.

PAGE 16: A red sun disk with wings is encircled by two protective cobras. The sun disk was associated with the mighty gods Ra and Horus, both falcon gods. The winged sun disk was often used as a protective symbol along the ceiling and above doorways in temples.

PAGES 22–23: Bringing gifts to the King: At the far right, the Pharaoh sits on his throne in a golden kiosk. He is wearing the blue war crown, traditional in New Kingdom paintings of this type, and is

holding in his left hand the symbol for life and the *sekhem* scepter, which means power and might. With his right hand he gestures "to summon." In front of the king, above, are cartouches (oval forms for the king's name) with the names of Senwosret III, the Middle Kingdom pharaoh mentioned earlier. (We do not know if Senwosret is the king referred to in this story.) Before the king, below, is a life sign, with human arms and legs. It holds a feather fan, and is fanning the king to cool him.

Our sailor stands before the king at the front of the line. He holds his hands up in a gesture which means "to rejoice," because he is happy that the king is pleased with him. Behind the sailor people are bringing the Serpent's gifts to the king: a woman carries a basket filled with gold rings, and is leading a baboon; a Nubian man leads a giraffe with a monkey, and four men carry a myrrh incense tree.

PAGE 25: Children were shaved bald except for one lock of hair on one side of the head. They were always shown naked.

ABOUT HIEROGLYPHS

Ancient Egyptian hieroglyphs are one of the most beautiful writing systems in the world. Hieroglyphs are made up of pictures of people, animals, plants, and objects, often beautifully rendered.

Hieroglyphs can be written in either direction, left to right, or right to left; and either horizontally or vertically, from top to bottom. Individual signs are always turned so that they look toward the beginning of the inscription. The hieroglyphs in this book are written left to right, so they are facing toward the left.

Hieroglyphs are not a simple alphabet, nor are they "picture writing" in the sense that the pictures always symbolize an idea. Some hieroglyphs represent an idea, and some represent sounds; many may represent a sound in one context or an idea in another. Usually the words are spelled out first in sounds, and then at the end of the word is an image for its meaning, called a determinative. Sometimes the determina-